T0146977

THE

DEVIL

IN ME

CARMINE TULINO

authorHOUSE®

AuthorHouse™
1663 Liberty Drive
Bloomington, IN 47403
www.authorhouse.com
Phone: 1 (800) 839-8640

This is a work of fiction. Names, characters, businesses, places, events and incidents are either the products of the author's imagination or used in a fictitious manner. Any resemblance to actual persons, living or dead, or actual events is purely coincidental.

Published by AuthorHouse 09/23/2019

ISBN: 978-1-7283-2888-1 (sc)
ISBN: 978-1-7283-2887-4 (e)

Print information available on the last page.

This book is printed on acid-free paper.

CONTENTS

The Devil in Me 1

My Mother was a Foster Parent 7

Just Being Kid's 11

Now Driving 15

To be Seventeen Again 19

Kenny's Place 23

Vito 27

Charlie 31

Tokyo 37

Europe 41

Being sexually abused has an effect on everyone differently, it definitely has a lot to do with the way a person lives their life, especially if they start getting abused at a young age it can alter their lives for the good or the bad. There was this kid that was living inside this older man's heart and soul and just ruined up his life completely, overpowering his deception in most of his life. In his 60 he can no longer live with himself being driven by this devil inside of him, losing everything. Hoping to find himself peace in whatever life he has left.

THE

IN ME

I was listening to an old man he was talking about his life, the road he went down. I was so compelled to listen, I asked him if I can write this all down and share with everyone. One thing he asked me was not to use any names and if I could do that it would be all right to share his life with everyone. So out of respect there will be no names in this book.

It all started when he was only 4 years old his mother at the time was pregnant and real close her water had just broke his aunt had come over to help, she only lived in the next building, and down town Brooklyn at the time was turning for the worst a lot more violence in the area. He went outside to sit on the front steps living on the first floor with the window open his aunt could hear him seating on the steps out front, she was there to help his mother, and she just started to go into labor. Outside in front of the steps were the two older boys from next door they playing in a big refrigerator box it looked fun they were calling him over to look inside, they were right in front of him so he put his head in to look inside when he did one boy pulled him in violently the other boy had his paints open the one that was holding him was a lot stronger and pushed his face down to the other boys open pants the two boys were black, stronger and bigger. They were so strong that he could not move they had him pinned down he started to scream and got away when he went inside crying his aunt yelled at him and told him not to go outside. He never forgot that. He said he could still remember how scared he was that day. Then he started talking about when he was about 9 getting close to 10 years old. Now the whole family moved to Bensonhurst he told me that his grandparents had bought a pretty big house his Uncle along with his aunt and cousin had moved in on the second floor it was pretty cool use to always ride down the block on his bike, he told me about this man who lived next door, that he was a cabinet maker he always was taking out wood to the garbage one day he had asked my new friend and his cousin if they wanted to make a couple of dollars by carrying the wood out to the front of the house so it can be taken away. It was pretty cool he would then tell us how they would just hang out after spending the money they had just made on things like candy and baseball cards. One day we saw the cabinet maker just hanging out smoking, then he called us into his workshop where he had a movie projector on the workbench, he said he wanted to show us something it was a rated x movie he told me that he and his cousin were so surprised, they never saw anything like that before. Then another time he told me about a time when he was just coming out of his grandfather's house this was some time after that movie incident told him to go down into the workshop to help him bring out some wood, it was nothing new about that he figured on making some money but when he went down the work shop he said it was real creepy the movie was already on playing that same movie. Now he told me what was real creepy was when he put his hand on his shoulder, now the cabinet maker was a real big guy and by him standing behind him there was no way out and his hand did not stop moving he told me he was real scarred he said it was the same creepy feeling he had felt before when those two boys attacked him in that big box it was a good thing that the film got jammed up that was when he left me ungraded and I ran out with his paints half way open, with no one to tell it was one more thing to keep in side to live with.

MY MOTHER WAS A FOSTER PARENT

His mother was a foster parent she took care of babies from the Goodie Angels Home his mother tried to take to take care of an older child she was closer to his sister's age and a little older than him she was in and out of foster home's a real troubled girl. That was after they had an infant baby die in his sleep. He told me that really scared the shit out of him. To see that baby just lying there not moving on his mother's bed that is why his mother wanted to take a break and try an older child. His mother did not know what she was getting into after taking care of 15 infants rising them from birth then putting them in their new home it was a good feeling knowing that you did something good. This old man told me things that this girl done with him and to him now he was a young kid. She did things to him that he saw the girls do in that movie to all the guys now he was just still a kid and not ready for all this. This set him off in the wrong direction still all of this for a kid to keep all this emotion building in side of him can make anyone not see life in it right settings, the way a young kid should be growing up and not feeling funny being just a kid. This poor boys mind is already destroyed and his life didn't even start yet. And it will get worst even just riding his bike around the neighborhood there was this alley way that they use to cut through to use as a shortcut to avoid all the fruit stands on the corner. One day while cutting through we heard a lady screaming from behind that big black door that was always bolted close, It was now open just enough to see that the lock was broke so just like curious kids they looked in and saw the lady screaming was a lady in a porn movie. That big black door was an exit to the Deluxe Movie Theater it showed rated X movies now all us guys that road our bikes through this short cut would stop and sneak in and watch whatever movie was playing. Now my new friend started to tell how he would talk the girls that hung out on the corner with us to take a walk and he would cut through the shortcut and sneak in and watch the movie with one of the girls that hung out whit us on the corer then take them down to his basement that is where his hang out room has and after watching that movie the girls would be the attacker.

JUST BEING KID'S

Now we were kids doing stupid kid things like the time we made a dummy and pretend to be fighting on the corner then throwing the dummy under the moving bus an scarring the shit out of that poor bus driver. Or there was this candy store on the corner of the of Bay 31 & Bath the owner use to pull the gate down and live the door open and finish cleaning the candy store he then told me that one hot night they put a lock on the gate and started to throw water balloons at the store and when he tried to chase us he couldn't get out he had to call his son to come and cut the lock. Now he would say that was crazy shit we did when we were young.

NOW DRIVING

I was talking to my new friend and you can tell he was real serious his eyes would tear up, and sometimes he would even cry a little and say wish I did not do some of the things I have done. But he would then say, I had a lot of fun doing the things I done.

He dropped out of school at the age of 16 started to work in a motorcycle shop, joined the karate school and got into weight lifting it's a good thing cause some of the kids that he hung out whit got involved with drugs most of them that did get involved whit drugs are now dead or they lived most of their life in jail. He was into building things like cars and motorcycles. He had just finished building his first car, and it was a Volkswagen. He went for a ride around the neighborhood driving down his block he meet his friend that lived on the block he was on his way to traffic court, he was a police officer just doing his job. My new friend had nothing to do so he drove him to court and was asked if he would pick up another officer this officer was a female officer a day in court was exciting being on the good side of things. The day was short but fun now driving them home they started to get real frisky, now they were both in the rear seat getting it on. he was looking in the rearview mirror and said to himself I'm not going to just watch so I drove down to Garrison Beach that were he would ride his dirt bike. I pulled over in the high weeds and we got out of the car and had the wildest time rolling around in the mud, the wildest sex ever, now after about 3 hours and all 3 of us covered in mud. They were going to the police officer house down the block from where my new friend lived, when they got there the police officers wife was walking down the block she got off work early he jump out of the car to meet her and my friend just drove the car into the garage to get out of sight now his brother used the garage as a body shop the female officer was waiting for the wife to go upstairs then he would drive her home. I left the car running and looked out to see if she went upstairs so I can leave and drive her were ever she had to go. One of the worker's was still working in the shop, now this guy was built like a big gorilla strong, This crazy ass jumps into the car that was running and fly's out of the garage not knowing what was going on and that she was a police officer thinking she a real slut, he told her that if she didn't give head to get the fuck out of the car he came back to the garage without her laughing saying what he had done. After that all hell broke loose being she is a police officer, she pressed charges against us but the only thing in my favor she did not know who he was, now he started telling me that he was only 16 years old and only had a permit to drive he was able to drive only whit another license driver which there was one present. His brother's body shop was where I built the Volkswagen, I told my new friend that must have been real cool having a car at 16 years old, he said don't forget my motorcycle. Well they never found out who the third party was and he never went to court.

TO BE
SEVENTEEN
AGAIN

Now at Seventeen he got his licenses but still not old enough to go into clubs unless some how he could sneak in but, there was always pretty girls walking around Fourth & Fifth Ave there was a club or a lounge almost on every other block and in the summer time you did not even have to go in a club or bar to meet someone. I was listening to my new friend with tears in his eyes just talking on about his past I did not want to go I just wanted to listen, getting back to him driving around Brooklyn with all the Clubs in the area he started to talk about the time he meet this real pretty girl by Spumoni Gardens seating there by herself eating a spumoni he told me that he seat next to her and started to talk, they talked for about one hour then they both went for a ride just around driving by all the clubs and just talking about every and anything when he took her home she asked him if he wanted to come in and hang out a little they both ended up in her living room and before you know it the close started coming off and also the Scotch came out whit shot glasses then in the middle of their wild sex her mother comes walking in the room he said being shocked and did not know what to do she calmly said, is it ok if she joins us she had a body just like her daughter and when she started, she had all these toys then it became a real fucking party that lasted all morning I felt thing that I never felt before all three of use covered in oil lived a fantasy. It was something that they were into whenever one would pick up a guy they just that bring him home and both have sex together with him but they never have a second meeting it was something between the mother and daughter.

KENNY'S PLACE

Now, It must be about a half a bottle of Scotch and he is still talking, I ask him what's with the name I thought you weren't going to use any names, all he said was aaaaaaah; And said we were all still young but don't forget I was still the youngest and beside going to the same club we were all well none especially me because I was working part time in The Leading Male clothes store the hottest clothes store in Brooklyn he told me when they were shooting the film Saturday Night Fever with John Travolta they clothes the store and bought all the clothes that was worn in the movie. And most of the bouncers bought their clothes there so they use to let me sneak in to which ever club they work at. Then he went back telling me about Kenney's place it was a meeting place usually on Friday nights after we all came out all clean after work to decide what Club or Bar we would end up going to. That night Kenney was expecting a female guest, now Kenney was the oldest the one that drove the big Caddy, the black Caddy! He was always saying how he was the best dresser and he was probably right well when Kenney's gest came walking through the door and he was trying to get rid of all of us, the exit was in the kitchen but he was still in the living room sweet talking and putting on his sweet charms you know there was no way he was not getting a piece of this sweet babe and when Kenney came back in the living room she had ask if he can stay and join us Kenney had no choice, he was already all over her, I don't know what kind of power he had but the girl would just love getting undressed for him and a lot more it was like he had a devil in him that commanded girls to do the unthinkable.

VITO

V ito was one of the worker from the body shop he use to enjoy going to a bar that was on 86st and 7th avenue the bar was called CARMINE'S one day he stopped in to see if there was anything going on, the bar was quit seating at the bar was Vito and he was talking to a girl and doing shots of Scotch. So he went over and joined them. He started to buy the shots of scotch after downing 3 shots each he ask if they wanted to go for a ride now he was driving and the girl was in the front seat and Vito was in the back seat he still had the Volkswagen we all started to get a little high from that scotch so he ask the girl if she had ever been in a real wine cellar when she said no that car went right to his house and all three went down in his basement Vito sat on the coach when he took her into the wine cellar tasting all the different types of wine he had in the wine cellar while she was tasting he started to taste her she stop and said what about Vito I said he won't mind I took her over to the coach made her sit in the middle and had another three some in his basement, all he said was she was not a quit girl had to keep something in her month to keep her quit and you know what that something was. Vito rest in peace.

CHARLIE

Now Charlie a real good looking guy that's how he started to tell me about Charlie all the girls were all over him he use to attract them and I would real them in for the kill even in school all the girls use to watch use play paddle ball and I would explain the rules to them. Charlie father owned an after hour Lounge it was small but had everything needed, pool table, juke box with good music small dance floor cozy little bar. On a rainy Wednesday night Charlie was cleaning up the place for his father, before the place would open. I would always walk over to hang out a little and sometimes give a helping hand. One night we had the door open with the music a little loud now the place would open late cause it was an after hour joint but now the music attracted when they look in to see were the music was coming from. My friend and Charlie started to talk to them telling them to come in and have a shot, we had a bottle of Johnny Walker Black opened on the bar we had got them to come in and have a shot or two then three. Then it was like a seen from Good Fellas my friend tells me that he walked over to the door then he locked the door and said now tour not going to leave he told me that he started to dance with two girls at the same time and Charlie started to dance with the other two, the only thing was my friends dancing was a little bit more touchy feely kind of dancing and started to undress them just when things were just started to get good Charlies father came walking in, now he is a big guy first he throw out the clothes then he threw us all out half-dressed. Two days later he told us what we did wrong and what we should have done right.

Now that the bottle of Scotch was getting real low, and just listening to him talk about everything and anything one thing I must of herd him say JO JOE over and over I finally ask him what is with this Joann he looked up that me stared me straight in the face and said JOANN, and just started to talk about a past summer I'm not sure which summer he has talking about it must have been back awhile cause he started to say. He would come home and jump in the pool so I guess it was in the summer still not sure how for back he was talking about what ever. You could her him ramble on talking about his sister also being in the pool with her girlfriend and that the girl friend was a feisty little thing always splashing water in his face or throwing the beach ball at him everyone could see she had a crush on him and she would always sleep over you know with my younger sister, now it just so happen that my sisters room was next to mine one night I got home it wasn't to late but it was hot out in the midsummer, going into my bedroom I would have to pass the bathroom and my sisters room when I got to the top of the step and turned to the right in the direction of my bedroom there was this perfect sexiest thing just standing in front of me in white baby dolls, with just the light on in the bathroom was on making her glow she just took control and grabbed my hand and walked into my room. After that all he would say was Joann over and over that was the start of something that went on and on she would always be sleeping over with his sister and in the middle of the night she sneak into his room. He was still working at the bike shop here the owner had a pretty big boat and use to keep it over at a yacht club with a big club house and always going there with my boss to help clean the boat everyone knew him one morning my boss got up and went to the store and never came back he had a villa over in Europe and a girlfriend and everything he needed his family went nuts for a while but that left the boat for him and Joann whit the yacht club and this big cabin cruiser it was 24 hours of nothing but sex, sex, and more sex and party and living nothing but the good life. Just as fast as good thing start they can end sometimes faster, he started telling me he sold a motorcycle to a friend, that friend was the owner to the body shop were we all hung out at and were he built his Volkswagen at after bringing the bike back to put headers on and new jets in the carburetor he took it for a test run and never came back, he got in a bad accident which put him in a comma for 3 months after coming back which was a miracle, Just like Christ getting up from the dead like nothing happen of course the body was all in pieces he lived in pain but there was no pain like the pain from a broken heart. Things were not the same as for Joann he never saw here or herd anything from her ever again.

TOKYO

There was a motorcycle seminar in Japan that he told me about was a trip he talked about meeting this girl her name was Fran he told me that she went 4 years at a collage in Boston and spoke 5 different languages she was leading the tour group he told me that she was perfect small with a great body he told me how he would not leave her alone talk her into taking him on a privet tour of Kyoto a little town outside of Tokyo and at night they went to clubs and go to special restaurants she was his personal translator for the three week that he was in Japan he never left her side he told me making love to a Japanese girl all they want to do is satisfy the man they are with and she did I told her if she would come back to the U.S.A I will marry her.

EUROPE

Four days after Tokyo he told me that they went to another cycle show in Germany, to look at different types of mopeds so they can make changes to the brand moped they were bringing in to the state. They were getting them from a cycle company in Milan. He told me how he and his friend hooked up with airline stewardess on the trip in from the U.S.A. to Germany. Listening to the way he would talk to the stewardess was unbelievable I don't know how he done it but he got them to take one week off so they tag along for fun to have fun. Then he told me about the train ride from Germany to Milan they were in one of those box cars that had sleeper cabins. Listening to what he was saying I don't know if the train was rocking from all the partying that they were doing.

Years and time went by that was when Scotch became his friend, the real miracle was that everything was still working and becoming more open when talking to girls about sex. Years went on and being exposed to sex at such a young age causing him to treat girls as a sex toy and never finding that special love who would put him in right direction till one day just sitting outside a club this angel just sat right next to him and started to talk to him and stayed even though he had a sharp and rude way of talking to her. This angel was perfect and stayed by his side for years he would tell me how much he loved her but there was this devil inside of him that made him talk to girls in a way, that one time he thought he was being a real cool and funny with all these jokes and saying thing that were really out dated but he was starting to sound weird. Times have changed and just passed him by with his body getting weaker and older. Now listening to him talk about how he wishes that he would have done or listen to that angel that was sent to him at a real time of need. Instead that devil inside of him had won. Now seating at this bar listening to him talk it must have been more than 3 hours then he got up and went into the bathroom and cried. Then I was talking to the bartender and he would tell me that was all he does ramble on about this angel then go in the bathroom and cry then come out and drink another bottle that poor guy is in so much pain. The bartender and I were talking for about 1 hour, it was a slow night then I said is he usually in there this long when the bartender went in the bathroom he found that poor man killed himself with a letter in his hand to this angel all it said was I LOVE YOU and that he was coming to see her so they can dance forever in heven.

THERE IS A SPECIAL ANGEL
THAT HEAVEN HAS SENT TO ME………………..
I CALL HER MY TRUE FRIEND

Printed in the United States
By Bookmasters